WELCOME TO
PASSPORT TO READING

A beginning reader's ticket to a brand-new world!

Every book in this program is designed to build read-along and read-alone skills, level by level, through engaging and enriching stories. As the reader turns each page, he or she will become more confident with new vocabulary, sight words, and comprehension.

These PASSPORT TO READING levels will help you choose the perfect book for every reader.

READING TOGETHER
Read short words in simple sentence structures together to begin a reader's journey.

READING OUT LOUD
Encourage developing readers to sound out words in more complex stories with simple vocabulary.

READING INDEPENDENTLY
Newly independent readers gain confidence reading more complex sentences with higher word counts.

READY TO READ MORE
Readers prepare for chapter books with fewer illustrations and longer paragraphs.

This book features sight words from the educator-supported Dolch Sight Words List. This encourages the reader to recognize commonly used vocabulary words, increasing reading speed and fluency.

For more information, please visit passporttoreadingbooks.com.

Enjoy the journey!

Cover design by Elaine Lopez-Levine.

Little, Brown and Company
Hachette Book Group
1290 Avenue of the Americas, New York, NY 10104
Visit us at lb-kids.com
www.despicable.me

First Edition: May 2017

Little, Brown and Company is a division of Hachette Book Group, Inc.
The Little, Brown name and logo are trademarks of Hachette Book Group, Inc.
The publisher is not responsible for websites (or their content) that are not owned by the publisher.

ISBNs: 978-0-316-50767-7 (pbk.), 978-0-316-50762-2 (ebook),
978-0-316-50764-6 (ebook), 978-0-316-50766-0 (ebook)

Printed in United States of America

CW

10 9 8 7 6 5 4 3 2 1

Passport to Reading titles are leveled by independent reviewers applying the standards developed by Irene Fountas and Gay Su Pinnell in *Matching Books to Readers: Using Leveled Books in Guided Reading*, Heinemann, 1999.

ILLUMINATION PRESENTS

DESPICABLE ME 3 ™

The Good, the Bad, and the Yellow

Adapted by Trey King

Based on the Motion Picture Screenplay by
Cinco Paul and Ken Daurio

LITTLE, BROWN AND COMPANY
New York   Boston

WHO ARE THESE FOLKS?!

Meet the **Minions**.

They are yellow, love bananas,

and work for super villains.

5

MINIONS

For years, the Minions searched for
the right villain to be their master.
They served a dinosaur, a caveman,

a pharaoh, and even a vampire.

But then they found Gru!

GRU

Gru was one of the greatest
super villains ever...
until he met three orphans.

They helped Gru learn that
happiness is more important.
Gru turned from "super bad"
to "super dad"!

Gru gave up crime to adopt orphans
Margo, **Edith**, and **Agnes**.

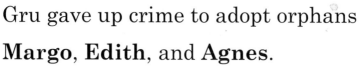

Then, Gru met **Lucy** and
joined the Anti-Villain League.
Lucy became his super-spy
partner and wife.
Together, they keep the world
safe from evil.

VALERIE DA VINCI

She is the new boss
of the Anti-Villain League.
And she is NOT nice.

After Gru and Lucy make a mistake,
Valerie fires them.
Then she throws them out of the blimp!

LUCY

Lucy is one of the world's best secret agents.
At least she was...until she lost her job.

If Lucy cannot be a perfect spy,

she can still be a perfect mother.

Lucy has three girls to keep out of trouble.

THE GIRLS

The girls lived in an orphanage
before they met Gru.
He needed to steal a shrink ray,
and they needed to sell cookies.
It turns out, they only needed
one another.

MARGO

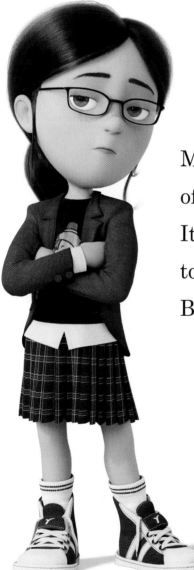

Margo is the oldest
of the girls.
It is hard for her
to trust people.
But she loves her sisters.

EDITH

Edith is the middle daughter
and often up to no good.
She loves a good prank and is
always ready to hatch a scheme.

AGNES

The youngest of the girls,
Agnes thinks of others first.
She sells her favorite unicorn
to help pay the bills.

GRU'S MOM

Gru talks to his mom.

He asks if he has a brother.

Gru's mom tells the truth.

When Gru's parents split,

they each took a son.

She says she got second pick.

MEL AND THE MINIONS

Gru is no longer a secret agent
or an evil criminal.
Now the Minions are left without
any mayhem.
Mel has an idea....

The Minions go on strike!
But when they cannot find dinner,
pizza leads them to trouble.

DAVE AND JERRY

The other Minions left,
but Dave and Jerry stick around.
So Gru puts them in charge.

They join the family
on a trip to Freedonia.
Freedonia has lots of pigs
and Gru's brother!

DRU

Gru has a twin brother!

Gru and Dru look exactly the same—

except Dru has beautiful golden hair.

He lives in a huge house
with his butler, Fritz.
Pig farming is the family
business—or is it?

BALTHAZAR BRATT

Who is this guy?
He was an actor
on an old TV show.
His show was canceled,
but now he is back!

Clive is Bratt's robot sidekick.

He plays the best '80s music.

Bratt wants to become the villain

he played on TV.

He wants to get revenge....

Bratt wants revenge on
Hollywood.

Will Gru be able to stop him?

Who will win?

Only the Minions
know—for now.
Just wait and see!

Attention, Minions fans!
Go back and read this story again—
but this time, see if you can find these words!
Can you spot them all?

bananas

dinosaur

unicorn

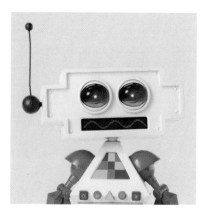

robot